CAN SOMEBODY PLEASE SCRATCH MY BACK?

written by Jory John   illustrated by Liz Climo

Dial Books for Young Readers

To Alyssa —J.J.

For Uncle Tim, Aunt Tweet, and Cousin David —L.C.

Dial Books for Young Readers
Penguin Young Readers Group
An imprint of Penguin Random House LLC
375 Hudson Street
New York, NY 10014

Text copyright © 2018 Jory John
Illustrations copyright © 2018 Liz Climo

Library of Congress Cataloging-in-Publication Data
Names: John, Jory, author. | Climo, Liz, illustrator.
Title: Can somebody please scratch my back? / written by Jory John ; illustrated by Liz Climo.
Description: New York, NY : Dial Books for Young Readers, [2018] |
Summary: "Elephant has a massive itch that no one can scratch, so Elephant is forced
to help himself—or so he thinks"— Provided by publisher.
Identifiers: LCCN 2017008132 | ISBN 9780735228542 (hardcover)
Subjects: | CYAC: Itching—Fiction. | Elephants—Fiction. | Animals—Fiction. | Helpfulness—Fiction.
Classification: LCC PZ7.J62168 Can 2018 | DDC [E]—dc23 LC record available at https://lccn.loc.gov/2017008132

Printed in China · 10 9 8 7 6 5 4 3 2 1

Design by Lily Malcom · Handlettering by Liz Climo · Text is set in Mikado

The illustrations for this book were done with digital magic.

ARRRRRRRRRRRGHHHHHHHHHHH

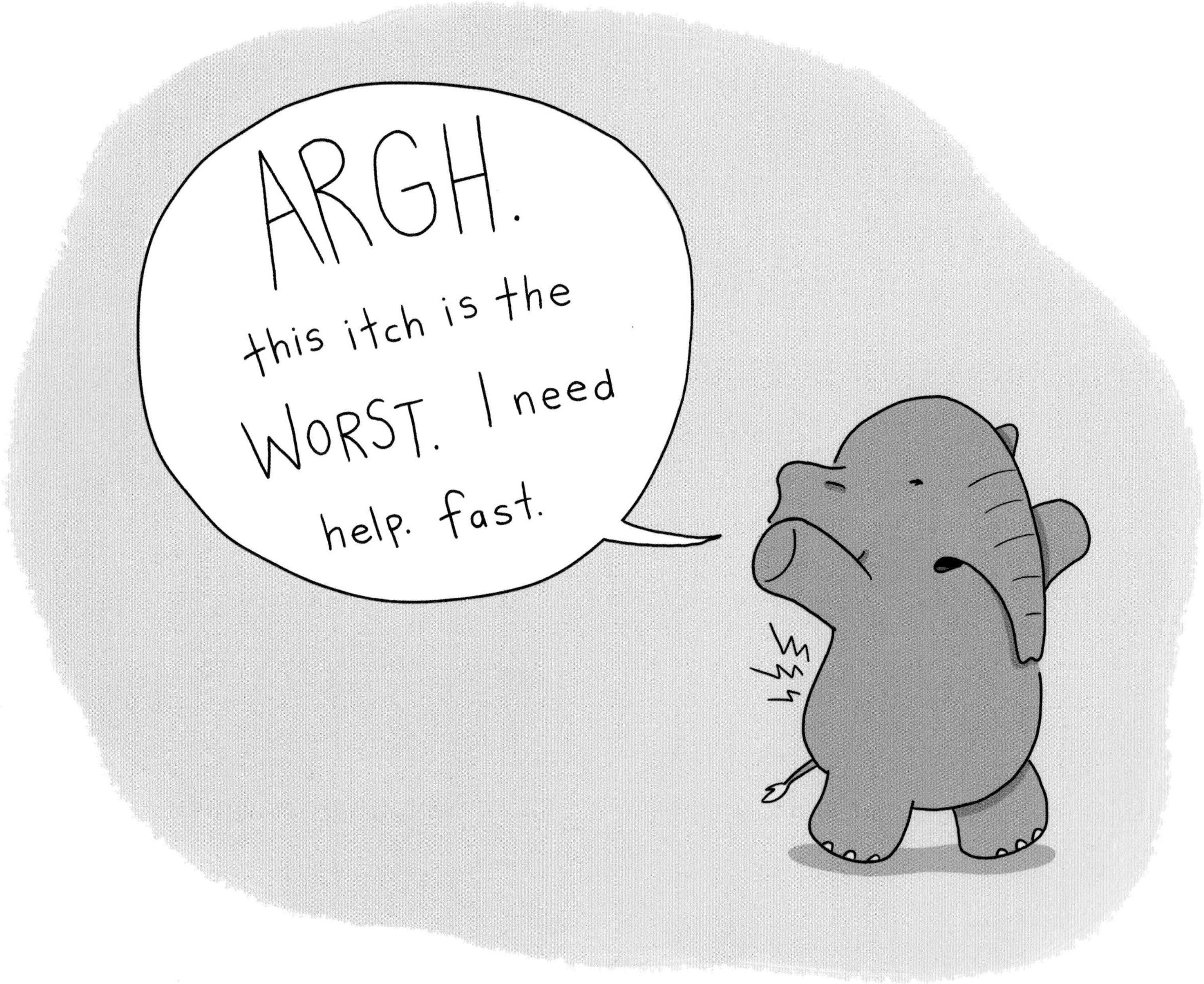
ARGH. this itch is the WORST. I need help. fast.

come back, meerkats!
THAT'S IT. WE'RE LEAVING.

oh, I have an itch on my back and it will never be scratched. I just don't know what to do.
sob

MYSELF

HERE?

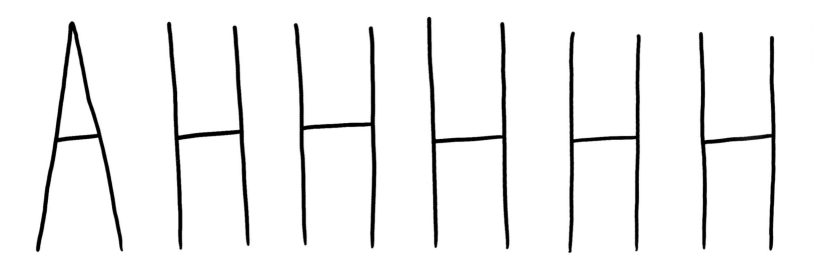